# The Last Whipping

## *Special Acknowledgements*

To Ron Hall, my husband, my encourager and Ouida McGinty, my editor, my mother.

# *The Last Whipping*

By Scarlette J. Hall

The Redhill Series
*Uplifting stories to make the heart merry!*

Copyright © 1989 by Scarlette J. Hall. All rights reserved.

No part of this publication may be reproduced or transmitted by any means in any form, electronic or mechanical, including photocopy, recording, or any information storage and retrieval system, without prior written permission from the publisher, except for brief quotations in reviews.

ISBN: 0-913507-12-1
Library of Congress Catalog Card Number: 89-085231
Printed in the United States of America.
New Forums Press, Inc., P.O. Box 876, Stillwater, OK 74076 U.S.A.

# Contents

Foreword . . . . . . . . . . . . . . . . . . vii
Chapter 1: Paddles and Peas . . . . . . . . .1
Chapter 2: Priest and Penance . . . . . . .9
Chapter 3: Picking a Penance . . . . . . 17
Chapter 4: Pressing Predicaments . . . . . 25
Chapter 5: Picking Up the Past . . . . . 31
Chapter 6: Peculiar Providers . . . . . . 37
Chapter 7: Piles of Postal Replies . . . . . 43
Chapter 8: Plethora of P's . . . . . . . . 51
Chapter 9: Payments and Promises . . . 61

## *Dedication*

To anyone who ever had to go forth to find a switch for one's own punishment.

# Foreword

In order that no one misunderstand or be offended, I must explain that some children are frightened by things with which they are not familiar. In fact, children will often scare each other with tales regarding the unfamiliar. Who was not told about the principal's electric paddle or the spooky old house on the edge of town? I remember the armored van which, unknown to me, came to our town to collect money from the banks. I was sure it was filled with criminals until the day I had to enter it on business. In this story, Gabey calls the Catholic church "creepy" simply because she is not familiar with the church which was set back in a copse of trees. It took courage for her to go to the church to carry out her elected mission, especially after the tales her friend told her. It is what she found there that is important.

S. J. Hall

*A merry heart doeth good like a medicine — may you, the reader, be blessed with a good dose!*

# CHAPTER 1

## *Paddles and Peas*

The principal leaned on his desk stretching his fingers to hold his weight. Gabey shivered under his lofty presence.

"In view of the circumstances, corporal punishment will have to be applied and your parents have concurred with the decision."

He took a large, ominous paddle from a hook on the wall and tapped it against the side of his leg.

"Hesitating, is he? Or just making me sweat?" she wondered.

"It's personally distasteful to me to have to use the paddle on an eleven year old—especially a young lady. You entered this school the same year that I came, 1947, and in all those years, I've never found it necessary to paddle a young lady. Do you understand why you are getting the swats? Answer me."

"Yes, sir. I called Loretta a 'one-eyed thing,' then I slapped her."

"Do you have anything further to say?"

"No, sir, 'cept I've had my bottom beat on before."

"Stand up and hold on to the chair."

Gabey heard the great swoosh of the paddle on the back swing. She bent at the knees and gritted her teeth. The first swat was always the worst. After that, numbness sets in as she recalled from experience. WHAM! It stung. Oh, my. It stung. Gabey swallowed. That sound, again, of the great swoosh and then a pause.

"Oh, no! He's taking his sweet time — letting my bottom warm up." WHAM! "Please God. Make him hurry," she silently pleaded.

A phone rang in the outer office. WHAM! The principal laid the paddle on his desk, and Gabey emitted a jagged little breath. Done. There was a knock at the door.

The school secretary poked her head in the office, flashed a quick, sympathetic look in Gabey's direction, and said to the principal, "A Mr. Ward is on the line."

"Thank you," he said. "Gabey, you can go on home. Your mother is expecting you."

Gabey walked home by herself, glad it was Friday, glad she got sent home, and did not have to go back to the last half-hour of class and be quizzed by everybody about the whipping. At least, the principal did not lecture her on how she should be a good example just because her daddy was a preacher. People seemed to forget that he was also a shade-tree mechanic. Facing mother and daddy was the next hurdle, especially daddy.

"I'm sure to have my tail beat on again," she thought, "'Spare the rod and spoil the child', and all that stuff from Proverbs. Seems to me they read it all wrong. They ought to be sparing with the rod and spoil kids a little. It says, 'Spare the rod.' Why don't they ever read it that way? I'm going to tell them that, too."

"Gabey?"

"Yeah, mom. I'm home."

"I'm out here on the back porch ironing. There is a pile of English peas out here I want you to shell before you do another thing."

Gabey put the bowl on her lap. Without argument, she shelled. Ping. Ping. Ping. The little green balls ricocheted off the sides of the metal mixing bowl. Mildred Hargus kept ironing. Gabey readied herself against the lecture that she was sure she was about to get. Chin lifted, eyebrows innocently poised, cool logic stored like arrows in a quiver, she decided, "I am ready for the persiflage. Neat word, persiflage." She liked words. Currently she was partial to "P" words.

"Big ones come in handy. If you can use a lot of big words in your arguments, people don't even know what you are talking about. 'Sides, big words scare some people off and intimidate others.

"At the very least, it makes them think twice and that gives you time to throw another one at them. Keeps them off balance in general. Words are weapons just as sure as hard clods are in a rock fight." So Gabey was armed and ready to explain all about the incident at school that resulted in a whipping, but her mother did not say a word.

"Lord, we thank You for the bounty, both on this table and in You as our Provider. Amen. Pass the peas, Gabey," her daddy said, handing her a platter of fried chicken. She took none. She did chase a few peas around her plate and drank her milk. Dinner continued. Nothing was asked about school.

"You aren't eatin' much, Gabey," said her daddy.

"Yes, I have."

"Don't dispute me."

"Sorry, I just meant I've had plenty," she said, bracing herself for the confrontation. It was difficult for Gabey to eat knowing a whipping from her dad would light up her bottom like a neon sign.

"If you're done eatin', help your mother clear the table so's we can get on down to the church and get it cleaned up for Sunday."

"Other churches have janitors. Why don't we?" Gabey asked.

"Can't afford it. It is better to be a doorkeeper in the Lord's house than a ruler in a rich palace. So get your brooms," he ordered.

Gabey did her sweeping as far away from her daddy as possible. "He's going to let me have it, but when? There is no way he'll let it all go by. It's positively torture for them to put it off so long."

"Gabey!"

Gabey jumped, her heart pounding in the base of her throat.

"This is it," she thought. "Yes, sir?" she replied.

Luff Hargus walked toward her with a slow, tired stride. "Take that wastebasket out and dump it when you finish these Sunday School rooms, please."

"Yes, sir."

The ride home was quick, but quiet. Gabey went to the shed in back of the house to replace the mops and brooms. Reluctant to go inside and face her folk, she sat down on the porch steps. It was one of those special nights — warm air weighted down with a mowed-grass perfume and insect songs. She wondered if insects liked "grass a la mowed." Dumb joke. She had always been able to cheer herself up before, but not tonight.

The screen door screeched. Gabey looked up at her dad. Tall, bony. No fat on him. Fat was a sign of laziness or gluttony, according to him. Besides, she suspicioned he fasted a lot. She was glad, actually, that he had come out to get it over with. It was better than sitting around in anticipation. Luff Hargus sat down on the step beside his daughter.

"Did you turn in your balsa wood bridge for science?" he asked.

"Nope."

"Why not?"

"Loretta Jones stepped on it."

"Why did she do that?"

"She said I took her spot on the display table."

"Did you?"

"I didn't think I had."

"And what then?"

"She smushed mine."

"And then?"

"You know what then. I slapped her and I called her a 'one-eyed thing.' 'Thing' wasn't what I was thinking. I kept that much to myself."

"Then what happened?"

"Old Mossback, I mean, Mrs. Moss, sent us to the principal's office. Loretta got sent home, and I got three swats. Three! It isn't fair. She gets by with murder just because she has a blind eye. Somebody probably poked it out one time because she is such a brat!"

"Gabey! Can't you drum up a little sympathy for anyone? What in the world is next?"

"The whipping you're going to give me is next, I guess. You always said if I get one at school, I get one at home. But I don't care if you whip me really hard. Jesus wouldn't let some one-eyed sinner get by with what a two-eyed sinner can't get by with, so whip me if you want to."

Luff propped his forearms on his knees, fingers laced together.

"Not this time. You are gettin' too old to whip. You need to do penance, and you are going to have to decide what the penance will be."

"PENANCE! That is Catholic stuff. We're not Catholic."

"Catholics have some very good practices to my notion, and penance is one. When you've done penance, something that really counts, I'll know it."

"Other kids get grounded. Other kids can't look at TV. That's their penance. We don't even have a TV."

"TV is an instrument of the devil," Luff said flatly.

"So is a table fork if you stab someone with it, daddy."

Luff Hargus stood up, still and quiet for a moment. "Gabey, you're uncommonly smart. Use some of your smarts and figure out and do a proper penance. Go on in now, and get ready for bed."

Before Gabey went to bed, she decided to look up the meaning of "penance."

"If I do decide to do a penance, I'd never tell him about it."

She sat on the edge of the bed in her nightgown, flipping through the "p" words, but some were not pleasant at the moment. "P" is for principal, p's for paddle, p's for peas, and p's for penance," she whispered to herself. Carefully, she read the definition, straining to find a loophole or an easy way of doing penance.

> Penance (pen'ans) N. 1. Eccl. A sacramental rite, involving contrition, confession to a priest, the acceptance of penalties, and absolution. 2. A feeling of sorrow for sin or fault, evidenced by some outward act.

Gabey studied the definition. "The stuff in parentheses is how to say it. 'N' is for noun. Eccl? That might stand for the book in the Bible, Ecclesiastes. A sacramental rite. That's like baptism and stuff. High church business, Confession to a priest? Absolution? What exactly is absolution?" Gabey asked. She quickly looked up the word. "Hm-m. Forgiveness, absolved by a priest."

"There's that priest business again. Creepy! I guess that means I'll have to go to that creepy, old Catholic Church and see a priest and confess. Maybe the priest can think of a penalty for me. If it's too hard, I just won't do it. Why, he might even absolutionize me right on the spot when he hears what a brat Loretta is. But I don't know about contrition. I've heard daddy preach on a contrite heart—being sorrowful for sin. I'm not sorry. I'm blasted glad I slapped her. I'd slap her again. She deserved it, so it wasn't sin in my books."

Gabey, thoroughly satisfied with herself, turned out the light, smugly fluffed the pillow and fell asleep, but not for long. She heard, "So Lord, I'm askin'. No, I'm begging."

Gabey sat bolt upright in the dark. "What on earth?" she wondered. She crept to the open window. It was her daddy walking the yard and praying. Gabey listened, but could hear only part of his petition.

"I've done all I know to do. If she's done wrong, it's got to be my fault. Punish me, Lord, not her. She ain't accountable. I'm accountable for her. I know You've required a man to be responsible over his own house and to keep it in good order. I'm concerned, Lord. I'm concerned about leading Your church, if I can't even keep my own house in order. Mostly, Lord, I'm troubled over Gabey. I don't know about girls. She's my main concern. I can do without a flock to lead, but I'm saddled with concern for that girl—." She did not hear the two words—"concern for."

Gabey ran back to bed. She buried her face in the pillow and covered her ears. She cried and cried. She loved her daddy and found it hard to tell him so.

"I always knew he wanted a son, and he's angry at me because I'm in trouble so much. I disgrace him and his precious church," she sobbed, "and for that, he doesn't like me. He thinks he is saddled with me, and now, he might leave his church and blame me for it. I'll see that creepy old priest. I'll see him first thing tomorrow. I'll do a penance. I'm not scared to do a penance, and daddy can keep his precious church for all I care—then he can't blame me if he resigns."

# CHAPTER 2

## *Priest and Penance*

Gabey popped a wad of bubble gum in her mouth to calm her nerves, like the baseball players do. She stuffed the definition of penance in her pocket and left the house letting the screen door bang behind her.

"Hey, Gabey! Where ya' goin'?"

"Oh, nuts!" she thought. "Beak Johnson. Thinks I've got nothin' to do but play catch with him."

"I'm running an errand for my dad," she yelled. "A partial truth is good enough for Beak," she decided.

"I'll go with ya!" Beak offered. He was throwing his baseball up like high, pop flies.

"Nope. You can't. This is private stuff," Gabey said, walking past.

Beak gawked after her somewhat surprised. She usually conned, wheedled, or otherwise tried to bring him in on everything she did, from mowing the yard to participating in her goofy adventures. Even last week, she tried to get him to help her spy out the janitor's boiler room at school. She was suspicious because the janitor hid a magazine behind his back when she went to borrow a broom for Mrs. Moss. Now she suddenly excluded him? Beak was unusually surprised and curious. Gabey turned around abruptly. "Hey, aren't you Catholic?"

"Sort of. Why?"

"What do you mean, sort of?" Gabey asked, her hands resting on her skinny hip bones.

"My aunt takes me there sometimes."

"Do you go to confession and stuff?"

"No way. I've heard the priest shuts sinners up in a black box dark as hell and keeps them there until they sweat their sins out."

"That's a lie, Beak." Gabey wasn't really sure. Pronouncing it a lie was her way of calling a possible bluff.

"Well, maybe they don't put ya' in a box, but they do stick you in a dark closet and make ya' cry and tell all your sins through a hole in the door. I saw it on TV."

"TV. All you know is what you see on TV," Gabey sassed.

"You're just jealous you don't have one."

Gabey ignored that comment. "Don't you know anything besides TV, like the priest's name at that church?"

"Father Andrew. Are you going to see him? That's where you're going, isn't it?"

"Did I say I was?" Gabey turned up her nose and continued on her way.

Beak, cupping his hands to his face, called after her, "They say he condemns souls to hell and gets drunk and laughs to celebrate while they fry-y-y!"

"Oh, shut up, Beak," she yelled back, "and don't follow me or I'll make sure you fry-y-y!"

"I can follow if I want to. It's a free country. And I will if ya' don't tell me what's up."

"I'll tell you when I'm ninety," she yelled back and turned the corner of their block.

Gabey tried not to be shaken by Beak's creepy stories, but they did nettle her nerves somewhat. She wasn't sure just exactly what to expect. Doggedly, she continued to walk toward the church, remembering her daddy's painful prayer, fearful of what could happen if she failed to do a proper confession and penance.

There it stood. The imposing St. Ignatius Catholic Church. A tall, grey stone building, smothered in trees and surrounded by shrubs. Gabey's heart pounded. She did not know whether to knock or walk right on inside. Perhaps it would be better to peek in first. One tug, two tugs. The door was either stuck or locked.

"Hey!" a voice bellowed and a hand grabbed her arm.

"Eek!" Gabey jumped and screamed simultaneously.

"What's going on here?" the black-frocked figure demanded.

"I — I came to see Mr., uh-h, Father Andrew."

"Oh, I see. I'm Father Andrew. For a moment, I thought I had a thief in hand. Funny to me why some people think there's money inside a church. We've had some trouble, you know. Someone did take our silver candlesticks. I was pruning the nandinas when I heard the doors rattle. Naturally, I couldn't help but — ."

"I'm sorry. I didn't know about all that."

"No matter. Now, what can I do for you, Miss uh-?"

"I'm Gabrieletta Hargus. But people call me Gabey."

"The shade-tree mechanics's daughter?"

"Yes." She liked him a little already for not calling her the preacher's kid.

"Your dad fixed our old church bus a few months ago. Good mechanic, Luff Hargus. He worked miracles on that old bucket of bolts. If he sent you here to collect, I'll have to beg for a day or two. We're embarrassed financially at the moment."

"I'm not collecting bills. I came for myself. I need to do a confession rite."

"Really? That's a bit unusual for a non-Catholic."

"Can you help me, please? It's real important."

"Yes, I can see it must be."

"Do you need to lock me in a box or make me cry through a hole in the closet? I'm not really very contrite. I might not even cry at all, even if you do lock me up."

Father Andrew laughed. Gabey did not see anything funny; in fact, she was hurt that Father Andrew was amused.

"Gabey, I wasn't laughing at you. I was thinking about a horrible, old movie I saw on TV recently about a mad, drunken priest hoarding money and terrorizing the parishioners, locking them into boxes."

"We don't watch TV. Daddy says it's an instrument of the devil."

"I think I take his meaning. And no, you don't need to get in a box or a closet, or even cry to confess. Tell you what. Let's go sit on the grass under that big silver maple and you can confess there. There's just one rule. You must be honest and you must be thorough."

Gabey related the whole story, the slapping, the whipping, her daddy's demand for penance, and his prayer for her accountability. She also told Father Andrew that she looked up the word "penance" and that was the reason she was there since priests hear confessions. At that point, she handed him the definition from her pocket.

Father Andrew chewed on the stem of a leaf and Gabey chewed on her bubble gum. He read her definition and she read him. He was not too creepy. His hair was barely gray around his ears. His hands were hairy, but his nails were clean. When he smiled, she knew he meant it. Finally, he stirred.

"You know what I think?"

"What?"

"You really hit Loretta where she hurts most by calling her a 'one-eyed thing.' She must be very self-conscious about that blind eye."

"But she gets by with everything because of that eye."

Gabey blurted, "She didn't get whipped. She just got sent home. They palliate her behavior. That isn't fair, and it happens tons of times."

The Father was surprised at her advanced vocabulary and was humbled. He was suddenly aware that he had considered people in small towns to be intellectually small. Instantly, silently, he asked for his own forgiveness for harboring such a prideful notion.

"Perhaps some do whitewash her offenses, and perhaps it isn't fair. However, we are doing your confession, so we must confine ourselves to you and your part in all this—not Loretta's. You are accountable for your actions, not hers."

"What, exactly, is 'accountability' anyway?"

"There comes a time when you must be responsible for your own actions. Knowing right from wrong, you are accountable if you choose to do wrong. The Church generally agrees that by age twelve, you would be able to choose, having acquired sufficient discernment."

"God doesn't love you after that, does He?"

"God is love. He especially loves children. He even sends angels to watch over them."

"I'm only eleven and a half. Do you suppose I still have an angel guarding me?"

"It's very possible."

"So I sort of get a free ride then until I'm accountable? Some angel is responsible for me until then? Daddy thinks he's the one responsible for me."

"Legally, he is."

"Do you think I'm accountable? I'm still not sorry I slapped Loretta."

"I can't say whether you've become fully accountable yet. You haven't understood the need to forgive; that's plain to see. You are somewhat contrite. Concern for your dad shows some contriteness. Understanding will come in due time, but you are off to a good start by being willing to learn."

Gabey looked at her definition again.

"Well, if I'm contrite and I've done confession, that just leaves penance. I'll do a penance and be finished with all this stuff. What penance do I have to do?"

"I can't give you one. You must honor your dad and think of one yourself. And Gabey, you can't race through absolution ticking off items like a grocery list. One must be patient and study, and grow up in discernment."

"I can't afford to be patient. I may be pronounced accountable any day now. Daddy could lose his church and I could go to hell, and it would all be my own fault. If my angel gives up and flies off, I'll be in a mess. Only, I'm not sure there really are any angels, real angels, walking around here. I know they came down and announced Jesus's birth, but no one I know has seen or heard from any lately. So they must have all gone back to heaven. Well, I've got to go," she said, shaking hands with the Father. "Thanks a lot."

"Ask your folks about angels, Gabey. Good luck and may God bless you." Father Andrew smiled from ear to ear.

"Where were you so long?" her mother called.

"Doing research. What's for lunch? I'm hungry."

"Hot dogs. Have one."

"Yea! M-m-m-m, they're good," Gabey said with her mouth full. The few peas she ate last night and the glass of milk for breakfast had worn off long ago.

"Another project so soon?" her mother queried.

"It's personal research. Mom, do you believe in angels?"

"I reckon. But the Bible doesn't say a whole lot about angels. One shouldn't rely on angels, but on the Lord.

Angels are messengers mostly. They work in the background."

"If I have an angel, he sure must be a shy one. Where's daddy?"

"He's already eaten. He's at his desk studying. Where are you going?"

"Out to play catch with Beak. I promised him. What is daddy preaching on tomorrow?"

"Forgiving, I think."

"I bet he gets all his ideas from watching me." Gabey had been convinced for some time that her dad preached at her from the pulpit. For that reason, she seldom listened to all he had to say. However, when Sunday came, she heard enough of the sermon to trigger her curious mind.

"Forgive everybody? Everything? Why?"

Her dad spoke out the answer as if he had heard Gabey ask it, "Bitterness can ruin your health and will steal your happiness. The devil would like for you to keep that poison pouring over your heart."

Gabey wondered how you do forgiveness. Just say it? That did not seem right, especially if you had to forgive a really mean person like Hitler. She doubted if anyone had ever forgiven Hitler. Old Mossback said last Friday during history that Hitler burned up Jews in big ovens. I think I'll ask Mossback if she's forgiven Hitler of his burning sins. What about the devil? Who's job is it to forgive him? Something was wrong with that notion, but she couldn't figure out what. She thought, "Probably because I don't have enough discernment. One thing for sure, Loretta is a snot and not any more worthy than Hitler of forgiveness. That's my discernment."

# CHAPTER 3

*Picking a Penance*

Monday morning held a rare surprise. Mrs. Moss ushered a new girl into their room.

"Class, this is Angelina Ward, a new student. I hope you will welcome her and make her feel at home. It's hard to go to a new school leaving old friends behind. Angelina, why don't you pick someone to be your temporary guide? Someone to show you to your classes and the procedure at lunch."

"I pick her," Angelina said, pointing straight at Gabey. Mrs. Moss was a bit surprised but quickly went on.

"Gabey, I hope you will take your duties seriously. It will depict good citizenship to be of helpful service to our newcomer," Mrs. Moss said stiffly.

Gabey enjoyed being picked, even if Mrs. Moss did not think Angelina chose wisely. Gabey was seldom picked by girls. Even though some liked her, she simply was not available. She preferred to play baseball during lunch recess with the boys. Mrs. Moss had suggested she quit that. It simply was not ladylike to squat behind home plate in a dress. Beak had a solution to that. He brought a pair of his knee shorts and kept them hid in his locker. Gabey wore them under her dress to play catcher. She had begged her father to let her have a pair of shorts, but

17

he said, "Absolutely not," and that it was improper for her to show her knees in public. Gabey insisted, all for naught, that if all those mamas could sit on the back pew in church baring their "bazooms" to nurse babies, she should be able to show her knees. Mildred Hargus had laughed but not her daddy.

Luff Hargus, flustered, had stuck his hands in his pockets and told Mildred it was definitely time to have "The Talk" about the nature of feminine matters. But that was a week ago and the slapping had caused her mom to forget the talk. Besides, Gabey did not intend to play catcher today. She had to show Angelina around school at lunch.

"Don't take more that you can eat, if you aren't sure you'll like it. They make us clean our trays before we can leave the table," Gabey advised Angelina.

"What's that?" Angelina asked, pointing to a soupy, odd-colored concoction. "It looks like cabbage and pumpkin all mixed together."

Gabey laughed when Angelina frowned and stuck her tongue out.

"It may be. When in doubt, leave it out. That's my cafeteria motto," Gabey replied.

"Mine is—if you can't name it or spell it, don't eat it." The girls laughed together and chose cheese sandwiches. Cheese is hard to ruin, they decided, and made their way through a maze of chairs, legs, and books to a table.

"Where are you from?" Gabey asked.

"All over. I've moved around plenty. Most of the time I get my schooling at home, but sometimes I get to attend school."

"Why do you have to move so much?" Gabey asked.

"My father lays rock foundations, so when the job is

done, we move on. Say, who is that girl?" Angelina asked, abruptly changing the subject.

"That is Low-ret-ta Jones," Gabey drawled.

"How did she lose her eye?"

"Who knows? She's a snot. You might as well know. I don't like her. She stepped on my science project last Friday and I slapped her jaws. I guess I'd had all I could stand of her. The teachers never see what really goes on around here. She gets by with everything because she's sneaky and doesn't get caught and because of her eye. I hit her because it was time somebody did. I know she steals stuff, but I can't prove it."

"Maybe she doesn't know any better," Angelina offered, "or maybe she is desperate."

"Forget her. Let's go outside."

Gabey and Angelina became close friends quickly in the next few days. Gabey found it easy to talk to Angelina about anything at all. They could look at each other and laugh. Angelina said her father had told her once that a merry heart doeth good like a medicine.

Some days after school, Gabey and Angelina stopped by the drug store fountain for a dip of the latest ice cream flavor. One time, Angelina would choose the flavor; next time, Gabey would choose. Today was Angelina's turn. The fresh peach was better than Gabey expected. "It's really good," she said.

"Mais oui! I ordered it, Gay-bee," Angelina said, with a French accent.

"Is that real French talk?" Gabey asked.

"Sure, I know a few words of French."

"I thought you said 'may we' until you said 'Gay-bee.' You're smart."

"So are you, Gabey. You're creative, too."

Gabey took another big bite of her ice cream.

"Miss Moss gave us a lot of homework, didn't she?"

Angelina said, shifting books aside for more elbow room on the little table.

"Yeah, good ol' Mossback."

"She's smart. Stiff, but smart."

"You know why our desks are all facing the north?"

"No, why?" Angelina asked.

"So we don't get 'Moss' on our backs." They giggled together.

"Miss Moss will always be safe from a rock slide. You know why?" Angelina asked.

"Why?"

"A rolling stone gathers no 'Moss'."

Gabey laughed with pure enjoyment. Angelina too. Their laughing and giggles were as contagious as yawns and itches. If one giggled, so did the other before she knew the cause of it. Often the mirth far outweighed the merit of the joke.

Normally, Angelina loved hearing Gabey laugh; it jumped in octaves and finished in a glissando. But today, as they sat on the porch rail at the Hargus's, Gabey's laughter was forced, more like a machine gun. Angelina could tell Gabey had something on her mind. Gabey's laughter was not "catching" today.

"What is the matter?" Angelina asked quietly.

"It's a long story."

"It's about Loretta, isn't it?"

"Sort of. How did you know?"

"Never mind. Just tell me."

Gabey explained about penance and how scared she was that her daddy might leave his church if she did not do a good penance, but she could not think of one. Furthermore, she might soon be accountable for her own soul and would go to hell if she died.

"I guess I'm evil," Gabey sighed. "Daddy gets all his sermons off my poor discernment. Even in school, I get 'I's' on my report card. Improvement needed. Only Old

Mossback makes one big 'I' down the whole citizenship column."

"You aren't evil. I can prove that," Angelina said with authority.

"How?"

"Go get your dictionary and your Bible." Gabey followed orders, bringing out her father's big Bible and her own dictionary. Angelina held up the Bible.

"Spit on it," Angelina ordered.

"What—spit on the Bible? Heck, no!" Gabey said.

"Why not? Are you superstitious?"

"No! Only ignorant people are superstitious."

"Then spit, if you aren't. Spit on all God's holy truth."

"I'm not superstitious; it's just that I don't believe in asking for trouble. I could spit on it if I wanted to. I don't want to, that's all."

"Spit on the dictionary then. It has the truth of words."

"No, that's my favorite thing next to my catcher's mitt. I'm not about to spit on it," Gabey protested.

"I'll tell you what I think. Only a really evil person could spit on the Bible and enjoy it. You respect the Bible, and even your dictionary. Since both have truth, you respect truth. That's not evil. Look; let me show you something else." Angelina took Luff Hargus's big Bible, laid it on the floor and stood right on top of it with both bare feet, toes hanging over the edge. Gabey had never seen anyone do that.

"My father said you can stand on the Word," Angelina explained.

"Was your father a preacher?"

"Not anymore, but he sponsors preachers. Come on; you try it."

Reluctantly, Gabey stepped upon the Bible. "This is weird. I can only do it because you said you can stand on the Word. I've heard folks say that, but I don't think they meant with feet."

"Yea!" Angelina yelled and clapped her hands. "You are acting in faith on God's word. You did it with your body; now all you have to do is do it in your heart."

"How do you know about all this stuff?" Gabey asked.

"My father made me do it once. Trust me. Hey! I've got to go. I mean, really go. But before I go, I have to tell you a secret. You can't tell anyone. Promise?"

"Okay, I promise."

"I found out how Loretta lost her eye. Her daddy often was mean from too much liquor and used to beat up her mother and Loretta when she was a baby. Isn't that awful? The mother died of Asian flu, so Loretta's aunt adopted her. Loretta doesn't even know she's adopted. That's part of the reason you can't tell anyone. Her aunt spoils her rotten trying to make up for all that. How would you like to be in Loretta's shoes?"

"I wouldn't," Gabey said, deep in thought.

"'Bye, Gabey. Good luck on doing a penance."

Several days passed before Gabey realized what Angelina had meant when she said she had to leave. She had moved — gone for good. Gabey could not understand why Angelina did not tell her she was leaving town. For days Gabey moped around, lonely and sad.

"Some folks don't like goodbyes, Gabey. It makes the sadness harder for them," her mother said. "In fact," she continued, pulling up huge clumps of crab grass, "one of the best things you can do when you are sad is to work so hard you drop. I'm sure you think that is a cheap way to get you to work. It isn't, really. What do you say? You can help weed these flower beds or sit there on the porch and be sad forever."

Gabey moseyed over to the flower bed and began to pull. Mrs. Hargus patted her daughter on the arm and tactfully left her to work alone. Angelina was the best girlfriend she ever had. It did not seem fair to have such a best friend for such a short period of time. With a fierceness, she uprooted dandelions and crab grass.

"Maybe she will write," Gabey thought. Straining at one long-rooted dandelion, in particular, she fell backward but it came out, roots and leaves. Work did seem to help. She decided if she ever had a business, she would hire the saddest people she could find. They could work hard until they dropped. They would be grateful, and she would be rich.

"Maybe Father Andrew could make some money for the church farming out people who need to do penances. It's too hard to think up your own penance," she decided. She set her mind to that problem again. Give her allowance to the Salvation Army? Lie on a bed of nails like a Hindu? Say the Lord's Prayer five hundred times? Didn't Catholics have to say "Hail Marys" until their jaws fell off?

Angry at not being able to think of something, she grabbed branches and shoved her way through a crepe myrtle bush to get at the farthest weeds. A branch flew back and smacked her squarely across the face.

"Ouch!" she yelled, backing out of the bush. Her face was scratched and bleeding. Immediately, she went to see the damage in the bathroom mirror. There was a small cut from the right eyebrow to the eyelid. She ran water on a wash cloth and bathed the wound.

"I could have lost my eye!" she realized. "Horrors! Then I'd look like Loretta. Ugh!" she thought, holding the cloth over her eye. Gabey wondered whether Loretta had an eyeball or not.

"An eyelid with no eyeball? That would look like a mouth with no teeth," she decided, shuddering. Wondering what it would be like to have one eye, Gabey took a bandaid and plastered her eye shut. The first thing she noticed was the annoyance of seeing the left side of her nose. Distances were harder to judge. She had to move her head more — right and left, and up and down — to take in areas her right eye would have seen without shifting her head. Wearing the bandaid was a definite nuisance. She lay down on the bed deciding to be still until the bleeding stopped. She tried to read as she rested, but it was a chore. She persisted, thinking she would get used to it. All she got for her persistence was a headache. She tossed the book aside and went to the kitchen for a glass of soda pop. She missed the glass on her first try.

"Rats!" she said and swabbed up the mess. "No wonder poor old Loretta is such a snot! One eye would run me nutty. Poor old Loretta," she thought, and yanked the bandaid off. She sighed, "That's much better."

"It's great to have two eyes," she said. "Loretta needs two eyes. That's it! That is it! I'll get Loretta a glass eye. She couldn't see, but she might feel like she could. At least, she might look better. But I'd better find out first if she wants one."

# CHAPTER 4

## *Pressing Predicaments*

On Monday morning, Gabey met Beak at his locker. "Beak, I'll catch for you today if you'll find out whether Loretta would like to have a glass eye."

"Do what? A glass eye! You're crazy. I'm not going to ask her that. Ask her yourself."

"I can't."

"Your mouth works. Why not?"

"I'll tell you why not in ninety years, I promise."

"Promise me a hundred dollars, I still won't do it. Never. No. Nix. Forget it, Gabey. I'll find another catcher today."

"You make me tired, Beak Johnson. You always want me to do stuff for you, but you don't ever do any stuff I ask," Gabey said. She turned around sharply and went to class. Beak knew she would not be angry long.

Mrs. Moss had another list of research titles on the blackboard. Gabey had decided long ago that Mrs. Moss's favorite assignment was research problems. The new topics were all about their town.

"You may be surprised at the interesting things you find out about Dispatch," Mrs. Moss said. Some of the students giggled.

"I'm well aware of the jokes and puns people make about our town because of its name. Other cities and towns are joked about also. Nevertheless, you can be proud of our town. It is a nice community. As you do your research, I trust you'll be even prouder. Furthermore, I want you to know this is a special assignment. The Chamber of Commerce is going to put together a brochure which they will take to their national convention. In it will be excerpts from the winning essay. First prize will be $25.00. A runner-up prize will be a new Esterbrook fountain pen. Look the topics over carefully and choose one."

Mrs. Moss always had more topics than students. That way, every one got a choice. She did not mind if two people chose the same topic. Gabey appreciated her being fair that way. Sometimes the topics sounded boring but turned out to be rather interesting once she got into the research. Loretta chose commerce and industry. That sounded very boring to Gabey. Beak chose architecture. Gabey settled for how the town and its streets were named.

Gabey shut one eye and tried to write down her assignment. She wondered again whether Loretta would like a glass eye. Mrs. Moss's voice droned on in the periphery of her consciousness. Gabey's mind wandered. "Maybe I'll win $25.00 in this contest. That ought to buy a glass eye. How much could a glass eye cost? Marbles only cost 50 cents a bag. It would take fifty hours of babysitting to make $25.00."

Suddenly, she realized she was being poked with a ruler. It was Mrs. Moss demanding an explanation for inattention. Gabey was momentarily befuddled, but quickly snapped into gear to explain her day dreaming. "I was so mesmerized by the portentous possibilities of my research topic, I failed to realize that you had proceeded to your eolian explanations, Mrs. Moss. I'm sorry," Gabey replied, plastering on a fake smile.

Mrs. Moss looked confused for a moment, then her

slight frown faded into disappointment. Gabey continued the phony smile. "Works every time," she thought. "Fling a few big words out and throw your opposition off balance. Words are powerful. Mrs. Moss would feel stupid to ask me not to use them. Even if she knows 'eolian', she won't know whether I've called her a Greek goddess or a windbag."

"Words," Mrs. Moss said sternly, "like forks, are useful implements for conveying nourishment or piercing the same."

Gabey missed the metaphor but was humbled by the logic. After all, she had used a similar fork logic on her daddy for a TV. Mrs. Moss was no dummy, Gabey had begun to suspect. In fact, she was gradually, if grudgingly, coming to respect her teacher. A twinge of shame crept through Gabey and victory in the word war lost it sweetness; discernment was taking root.

The new assignment was going to take up much of Gabey's spare time — time she needed to figure out how to get a glass eye for Loretta. How much could a glass eye cost anyway? She determined to find out right after school.

Dispatch had no eye doctors. The racket store, their name for the local five and dime, sold eye glasses out of a bin for $1.98 a pair, but they did not carry glass eyes. Gabey took off for the Smith Funeral Home. The funeral director had a telephone directory for Fairview, a larger town thirty miles south of Dispatch. Her daddy had borrowed their directory before to locate special parts for old cars. Mr. Smith, the owner, took the directory from the bottom drawer of his desk. He looked like a painted, cardboard cutout to Gabey. Not a hair out of place. Clean, even fingernails. No wrinkles in his suit or face. Stiff starched shirt. Stranger still, he appeared comfortable all pasted together.

"Your dad needs parts?" he asked.

"No, sir. I'm doing a school report and need to find out something. I've got a dollar. Can I call Fairview for a dollar?" Gabey queried.

"Shouldn't cost more than 35 cents. Is your home phone out of order?"

"No. But if you don't mind, I'd like to call from here before I go to the library."

"Fine," he said. Mr. Smith left the room puzzled at the reasoning of children's minds.

"Fairview Eye Clinic. May I help you?" the voice said.

"This is Miss Hargus," sounding as prim, grown up, and businesslike as possible. "I'm doing a research paper and I need to know the cost of a nice glass eye." Gabey wondered if the owner of the voice was laughing.

"Just a moment — please — I'll have to look that up." Gabey waited.

"Miss Hargus?"

"Yes."

"They range in price from 500 to 700 dollars." Gabey gulped, stunned. The icky perfume of carnations and Mr. Smith's lingering, spicy aftershave closed in on her.

"Miss Hargus? Did you get that?" the voice asked.

"Uh-, yes. Oh. Thank you very much," she said, hanging up slowly. She laid 40 cents on the desk and left. "What in the world were glass eyes made of, for heaven's sakes?" she wondered as she walked to the library. "I've never even seen a hundred dollars all in one pile in all my days. How on earth can I scrape $500.00 together? I'll have to do some tall thinking."

Gabey pushed through the revolving door of the Carnegie Library. There were two books which she checked out on the origin of personal names, but she found nothing on how the town was named. Gabey walked home writing down the names of streets. All presidents or trees. "Big deal," she thought, "our street names are so unoriginal."

By the time she turned down her street, Gabey could smell something wonderful. Before she reached the porch steps of her home, she knew what it was. Her mother was making strawberry jam. That meant a cobbler for supper out of the overripe berries. Gabey set her books on the kitchen table. There sat the cobbler, fresh from the oven.

"You can have some fresh berries, but no cobbler until after supper. How was school?" her mom asked, stirring a pot of steaming jam.

"Okay. I have to find out how Dispatch and the streets got named." Her mom laughed lightly.

"How did Dispatch get it's name?"

"I don't know yet. All I know is that every time you say it in a sentence, it sounds like a corny joke." Gabey popped two perfectly red strawberries in her mouth and looked through the mail on the table. No letter from Angelina.

"Mom, who would know how this town got its name?"

"Oh, I don't know. Why don't you run next door and ask Mr. Johnson?"

Mr. Johnson, Beak's dad, had worked for the Weekly Dispatch for thirty years, if you count his time as a paper boy. Mr. Johnson said he thought the town was named after the paper. Mr. Tom Browning printed a paper of sorts before the town was incorporated and carried it himself to the neighbors. Mr. Johnson drew her attention to one of those old papers which was framed and hanging over his desk. Gabey took a good look. It wasn't any bigger than a page out of a Big Chief tablet. That was odd. She thought all papers were 28 inches wide.

"Who was Mr. Browning?" Gabey asked.

"He owned all the land where this town now resides.

He named the paper 'Dispatch.' It listed grain prices, trade and auction news, and the latest news from the reconstruction government. That wasn't but a few years after the Civil War. Look at the date."

"Wow! 1872," Gabey said.

"Mrs. Clover may also be able to give you some information. She's nearly ninety years old, but she might be able to tell you something."

"Who is she?"

"She is the old man Browning's daughter," Mr. Johnson answered.

Gabey took a closer look at the newspaper on the wall. Then, a second look. Her eyes popped open wide. There was the answer to her money problem right on the front page of the old "Dispatch." A plan plainly unrolled itself in her mind. Tomorrow, she had two things to do, and one was to pay a visit to Mrs. Clover.

# CHAPTER 5

## *Picking Up the Past*

Mrs. Clover lived in a gingerbread trimmed, white framed house not far from school. Gabey made a mental note to point out all that curlicued work to Beak. Mrs. Clover was on the porch in a rocker, her lap covered by a wool afghan in spite of the warm day.

"Mrs. Clover?" Gabey asked.

"Well, looka' here," she answered sweetly and surprised.

"I'm Gabrieletta Hargus. Can I come on your porch and ask you some questions?" Gabey asked. "I'm doing research."

"Come right on up here and ask away. I love to have young 'uns visit."

Gabey opened her tablet and prepared to take notes. "Mr. Johnson, he works down at the Dispatch, said you might be able to tell me exactly how this town got its name. He said it was named after the paper."

Mrs. Clover raised her eyebrows up high. She smiled and nodded slightly. "Funny. I can recall that story well, but I can't remember what I ate for breakfast," she laughed. "Well, most folks think this town was named after the paper, but it wasn't. It was named after a horse. You're Luff Hargus's young'un, aren't you?"

Gabey nodded yes. Mrs. Clover was not asking, simply putting two and two together. "Your papa is a fine man. He comes here regularly. Nailed my mailbox up last time. It's getting old and falling apart a piece at a time, just like me. We're running a race to see who will last the longest," she chuckled.

Gabey sensed two things: a sharp mind under that thin, frizzly topknot, in spite of her rambling; and her daddy got around more than she knew.

"Mrs. Clover, you said our town is named after a horse?" Gabey reminded.

"Wanderin' from the subject, am I? Well, not really. I wasn't sure I wanted to tell you. But somebody ought to know. I've kept shut on the subject for all these years. I was skeptical of the story at first — thought it just a family yarn, not something a body wants to tell around. But now, well, 'tisn't a yarn. It's true. I've lived long enough to know 'tis so, and time someone else knows it, I reckon. Are you worthy?"

"Worthy? I don't know. But I sure want to hear the story. That's what I came for."

"Then it's a sign to me you are worthy. Don't interrupt me now, or I'll forget where I left off."

"Okay."

Gabey saw Mrs. Clover's eyes take on a faraway look as she began her story.

"Maxwell Fairview took the land you are now standing on at one time. Used to be Browning land. He bought it up for back taxes after the Civil War. Parceled it out to sharecroppers at nine to one. He got nine parts of all produced. My folks got one part as sharecroppers on what they once owned. My papa was just a lad of fifteen. The Civil War hadn't been over long. Times were bad for everyone except the scalawags and Yankees and men like them. About the only thing of any worth they had left was a fine, thoroughbred horse called Dispatch. He was fast and beautiful, and my papa loved him. Fairview wanted that horse. Offered to buy it. He had a passion for racing. But my papa wouldn't sell. You see, the horse had been a present from his papa and all he had left to remember him by—him dying in the war and all.

"Fairview made a final offer. They had to take it or get off the land by the end of the year. Fairview claimed they weren't making him enough profit anyway, and took on about how generous he'd been to let Granny and Papa stay on. There had been a bad drought. The only things that grew were a few vegetables in the garden which they sold for a few coppers and kept growing by hauling water until the well was nigh on to dried up.

"Times got worse. The end of the year was near. Finally, my papa went to Mr. Fairview and offered to race for him. If Papa won, he'd give his horse to Fairview along with all the winnings in exchange for the deed to all the former Browning lands."

"Your folks used to own this land before Fairview?" Gabey asked.

"Yes. If Papa lost, he was to sell Fairview the horse for a grubstake and leave the county. Either way, Fairview got the horse. Greedy man that he was, he accepted Papa's offer. Anyway, Fairview owned other lands and property to the south where the town of Fairview is today. The farms where our town is weren't prospering him much. Now, it so happened that Papa had let an old, wandering Negro day-worker, called Hydro, sleep in their barn. Papa fed him, not leftover pickings, but the same as he and granny Browning ate. Granny found out about Hydro eventually, but she wasn't angry. She told Papa to see to it that Hydro had a blanket and a pillow, too. Hydro came and went. He'd be there sometimes and gone sometimes."

Mrs. Clover pulled off her glasses, pulled out a hanky, spit on the lenses, and wiped them clean.

"Papa liked to talk to Hydro since he didn't have his papa to talk to. Right after Papa told Fairview he'd race, Hydro came back. Papa said old Hydro told him not to mind losing Dispatch. Dirt would last far longer than a horse. He said it was fine and noble to give up something you love for a greater good. That cheered Papa a bit, because the original Browning lands enclosed at least ten other sharecropper holdings. Papa had in his mind to give the other farmers clear title to those farms. He loathed keeping it and turning into something as greedy and ugly as Mr. Fairview was.

"Granny Browning agreed. Those farmers had helped her out many, many times. Granny and Papa figured they could make out fine not having to pay Fairview 90 per cent. They prayed and decided they'd stand on a faith foundation whichever way the race went. So they did. Papa won the race easily. The neighboring sharecroppers got their deeds and pretty soon, things began to turn around. Papa said as he lived and breathed, it would cloud up and rain in these parts on Browning holdings, while the rest of the county parched and curled up. All the neighbors helped each other with the good harvest.

"Papa started up a paper called 'Dispatch', after the horse which made their good fortune possible. It kept all the neighbors informed on trade prices and the market news, in general. As the area prospered, a mill was built. The town grew up around it. Papa put his newspaper in town. When the town incorporated, all the local farmers agreed to call it 'Dispatch' after the horse, not the paper. There was a big celebration. Old Hydro called my papa aside after the incorporating, and said, 'You're a good man, Tom Browning. The town is built on a good foundation. Nothing evil will be able to tarry long in it. Like Dispatch, good would be dispatched from Dispatch, and be prosperous.'"

"And that's the truth, Missy."

"What happened to old Hydro?" Gabey asked.

"He hauled water to Fairview till the drought broke, then he moved on. No one saw him leave," Mrs. Clover replied.

"Old Hydro missed it though," Gabey said. "After all, this is just a little-bitty old town. It doesn't look very prosperous to me."

"Depends on what you mean by 'prosperous'. Don't you see, Missy? There's no sin den to keep ugliness here. Nothing here to attract the little-bitty mean folks. Not that we're all perfect in Dispatch, mind you. The good people who do leave here go with good inside them. Folks who move here sweeten up or move on. Old Hydro's blessing was a true one, all right. I've watched them come and go."

"Who?" Gabey asked.

"You'll find out, Missy. Guess I sound creepy, huh?"

"I was just thinking that," Gabey blurted out before she clapped a hand over her own mouth in embarrassment. "I didn't mean you are creepy. I use that word too much, according to my mama."

"It is a strange story—borderline creepy, perhaps, but I'm not daft. What I've told you is so," Mrs. Clover laughed. "I was told you call things 'creepy'. There aren't really any creepy things in this town, only things you don't understand."

"Yeah, like that old Catholic church. I used to think it was creepy. Did my dad tell you I say 'creepy' a lot?"

"No. Angelina did." Gabey's eyes flew wide open.

"Angelina! You knew her?" Gabey asked.

"She came by one day. Wandered up on the porch

here to visit. Brought me this pretty afghan. Lovely, isn't it?"

"Do you know where she moved to, Mrs. Clover? I'd love to write, but I don't have an address. They don't even have one at the school. Do you know where she is?"

"I haven't a notion. They come and they go all the time." Mrs. Clover quickly changed the subject. "Hand me that seed catalog, Missy, and those glasses. Jesse Wash is going to plant me a new rose bush when I get it ordered." Gabey did as asked.

"These glasses cost me a quarter," Mrs. Clover said, wiping them again and setting them on her nose. "Got them at the racket store twenty years ago. They're up to $1.98 now. Everything's high as a hog's back." Mrs. Clover peered over the glasses at Gabey. "You're uncommonly smart, and a good child. I use glasses for print reading, but I don't need them for people reading. Furthermore, what I told you about Dispatch is the plain truth and I know you are worthy. You'll find out," Mrs. Clover said convincingly.

"I do believe you. And thanks. It really will make a good report. I hope to knock their eyes out with my story."

"Oops!" Gabey thought, "wrong choice of words. Eyes got me into this mess." To Mrs. Clover, she said, "I have to go now. Maybe I can come back sometimes."

"You come on over anytime. Tell your folks, 'hey'."

"Yes, ma'am. 'Bye, and I'll be back real soon. Thanks."

One job done and one to go. Gabey wasted no time getting to the racket store and home again with an extra large package of typing paper. First, she opened the Bible and found a chapter to verify her next move. Gabey grinned. Next, she went to her daddy's study desk, pulled out a ditto master and began to type with two fingers.

# CHAPTER 6

## *Peculiar Providers*

LAST CHANCE! INVEST ONE DOLLAR FOR A GUARANTEED THREE TO POSSIBLY 3 HUNDRED PER CENT RETURN ON EACH DOLLAR INVESTED
    SEND TO: FUTURE   INVESTMENTS UNLIMITED
                 C/O 128 PIERCE STREET
                 DISPATCH, OKLAHOMA

Gabey ran off fifty copies and mailed one to every family in her father's congregation. If it worked, she would get another mailing list from the court house and mail out some more. She felt great! All her problems were solved. Grabbing the catcher's mitt, she ran outside to hunt Beak.

She told Beak about the gingerbread trim on Mrs. Clover's house. Beak said he'd been looking at the old business buildings on Washington Street. Most were Romanesque or post and lintel designs. Beak waited for Gabey to be impressed with his architectural language. He couldn't tell if she was or not. He had not thought about including regular houses in this research, except the one where Angelina had lived.

"It has strange architecture — mixture of styles from add-ons — a perfect example of change in times, a long history," he explained to Gabey. "It was first built by Ethel Pergola during the depression. She had money from somewhere, at least, enough to run a soup kitchen and free rooms during the depression when times were so bad. It then changed hands to a Joe Claire, who turned the place into a used car lot. He went broke. Too honest and an easy touch. My dad remembered him. When he left town, your friend, Angelina and her father occupied the place as a home. Now, a Negro man, Jesse Wash, lives there. He hauls off junk, and does day work when he can get it. I talked to him and asked him if I could take pictures of the house. He is a good ball player. He plays with the kids at the park. Jesse showed me some slick grips. Watch this." Gabey nearly missed the ball which took a sudden dip.

"Wow!" she said, "Great pitch!" Beak tried not to look too proud.

"How did you find out about all those owners?" Gabey asked.

"The abstract office. Daddy said they'd have all the titles and deeds, who owned them and how much they'd paid and everything," Beak explained.

"Wouldn't it be something if one of us won the $25.00?" Gabey remarked.

"Yeah, I'd buy some new baseball shoes. My feet are growing so fast my toes hurt in these."

Gabey threw a side arm pitch. "Well, I found out this town was named for a horse. Can you believe it?"

"Why not? It's a one-horse town," he said, laughing at his own joke, and practicing his drop-ball grip. "But I thought it was named after the paper."

"No. I'll tell you the story later. Something is creepy about those names you mentioned. Pergola rings a bell. Some of those people sure have off-beat names. Ethel Pergola That's a 'p' word, and it's familiar, but I can't place it. Hey! I checked out two name books from the library. They're in the house. I'll get them." Gabey was so enthusiastic that Beak went along with the idea. Gabey returned with the name books and her dictionary, and they set out to determine the meaning of the names.

"Ethel, Ethel. Here it is! Ethel — noble one. Pergola — not in the name book. It's here in the dictionary. Pergola is an arbor, especially one with a roof supported by columns, vines growing on it.

"Jesse — (Hay-soos); Spanish for Jesus. Jesse. Semitic house."

"Wash — no Wash mentioned in here. Maybe it means what it means."

"Joe — from Joseph. Semitic."

"What's Semitic?" Beak asked.

"Descendants of Shem," replied Gabey.

"Oh, that explains everything," Beak said sarcastically.

"Shem was one of Noah's sons. You know, Noah of the ark. Claire — one who discerns." Gabey closed the book and began to twist her pony tail. "Oh, my! Oh, my gosh! Oh, gosh! Old lady Clover, she knows! Oh! I don't believe it. I DO believe it! Beak, you'll never believe it!"

"Mrs. Clover? What do you mean? All I know is you're looking up names. You won't tell me what is going on till you're ninety, right?"

"Wrong, Beak. I'm going to tell you right now. Only you are going to have to help me prove it. Brace yourself, Beak."

Gabey explained. "All the residents of that house came to town and left again. No one knows where they came from or where they go. Mrs. Clover said they do it all the time. Their names are all Biblical names, or made-over versions of the same, or names suggesting Biblical stuff. They won't use worldly names, Beak. You know why? Because — get this! they are all angels!"

Beak cocked his head and backed away. "Angels! Call the men in the little white suits." Beak fluttered his fingers. "You've flipped. You're gone." Beak said in a singsong voice.

"Now wait a minute; listen up. That's why Angelina won't ever write. She's an angel." Beak rolled up his eyes.

"Old Hydro was the first angel around here, probably," Gabey went on.

"And who is Hydro?" Beak asked sarcastically.

"He was an old Negro angel acting like a day worker. He probably blessed this town because Mrs. Clover's papa was good to him, and to the rest of the sharecroppers who lived here then. Angels can't really interfere unless they have some sort of special directions. They are messengers, and all they can do is suggest stuff and keep in the background. But prayers are like legal documents that give them permission to really do things faster, I think. I'm not real sure. But ever since old Hydro blessed this town, the angels have guarded it. That house of Ethel Pergola is their headquarters. Ten to one says Jesse Wash is an angel. Everything the angel-people did matches their names. Ethel Pergola, a noble person, providing a roof, or pergola, over the heads of hungry people back in the Depression Era. As for vines on the roof, the Bible is full of stuff about vines. John 15 is full of vines. Joe, like in Joseph in the Bible, who could interpret dreams and prevent bad stuff from happening, probably made sure people got the cars they needed for some special reason known only to him. I'll bet he could see their needs — clairvoyant — Joe Claire. Get it?"

"That's stretching it, Gabey," Beak replied. But Gabey paid no attention.

"And Jesse is for Jesus, and Wash, wash is for cleanse. That's what THE Jesus does and Jesse is here on a cleaning mission, I'll bet a nickel. Someone has asked for help and Jesse is here to see to that help. When he is done, he'll fade out of sight just like the others."

"Your name is Gabrieletta, after the angel Gabriel, and you certainly aren't an angel. You are trying to make something out of nothing, and it's weird," Beak replied nervously.

"Yeah? Well, your name is Beacon and you don't shine. We are just people. They are angels. Even Mrs. Clover said 'they' come and go. I'll bet she knows they are angels. She even knew Angelina. They are probably nice to her because of her daddy."

"If Angelina was your so-called angel who won't interfere until asked, who asked? Did you pray for help?" Beak cross-examined.

"I didn't ask. Daddy did. I heard him one night. Hey, wait! I did sort of pray when I got my last whipping. I said, 'God, help!' I meant it, too. The principal was taking his time to let the sting wear off between swats. I remember the phone rang and he hurried it up because a Mr. W-A-R-D was on the line. I was the ward of an angel, Angelina. Ward — can't you understand that?"

"Coincidence," Beak said.

"Yeah? Did you ever see Mr. Ward? I never did. That was Angelina's last name. She was my angel, don't you see? The father she talked about was God Himself Who lays foundations — not brick ones — living ones. So, I was her ward. She suggested lots of stuff to me that no one our age talks about. She even tried to get me to spit on the Bible to prove I wasn't evil."

Beak threw up his hands. "Spit on the Bible! There you are! No angel would ask you to do something like that. What if you had done it? She would have been in a jam if she were an angel."

"That's the whole point! She stuck her neck out for

me, like a dutiful guardian would. She proved I wasn't evil because I couldn't spit on the Bible."

"Angels," Beak said, "are supposed to have wings. Angelina didn't have any, so that leaves her out; and they are pure-dee white in the face, so that leaves out Jesse Wash. He's so black, he shines."

"Hooey! Angels can be any color they want, I'll bet. Did you ever see an angel with wings? Someone just made that up for Christmas cards. I've never heard of wings on angels in the Bible. Seraphim and cherubim have wings, not angels. I ought to know. I've been to preaching three times a week since I was born. You don't go, so how would you know?" Gabey retorted.

"Angels with wings are on the stained glass windows at the Catholic church. I saw them when my aunt took me. Why would they put wings on angels if it weren't so?"

"I don't know. Ask Father Andrew. But wings or no wings, I'll bet if we tail Jesse, we'll find out he is an angel."

"Not me, no way. You are full of peas in more ways than one. Just count me out. He's a good ball player, but probably straight out of prison, not heaven. My advice to you is to get your head screwed back on. Go take an aspirin or something," Beak said, pointing his finger right at Gabey's nose. He walked across the yard and squeezed between the hedge.

Gabey frowned. Beak had no sense of adventure. She took her books into the house and reminded herself to go to Mrs. Clover's on Saturday morning on very important business.

# CHAPTER 7

## *Piles of Postal Replies*

Mrs. Clover was on the porch of her home at 128 Pierce Street. Gabey opened the mailbox by the yard gate. Nothing in it. She was surprised.

"Not nice to open a body's mailbox, Missy," Mrs. Clover called from behind her new, white hybrid rose bush. "Federal offense, actually."

Gabey wondered that she could see so well through twenty-year old, twenty-five cent glasses. "No mail for you, Mrs. Clover," Gabey said innocently.

"There has been plenty of mail today. Maybe you know what is going on."

Gabey reddened.

"Out with it, Missy." So Gabey confessed she had used Mrs. Clover's address to raise money for a glass eye for Loretta; that she wanted to keep it a secret from her daddy since he said he would know if she did a penance.

"But how do you plan to live up to your promise to pay the returns on the money?" Mrs. Clover asked with concern.

"I'm not. I looked in the Bible. God says He will. Some will get threefold return, some a hundred. *I* didn't promise anything. I only sent offers to people in my church who say they believe the Bible," Gabey explained innocently.

*43*

Mrs. Clover started to giggle and then laughed hard, wiping tears out of her eyes. Gabey laughed too.

"What a hoot! You certainly have permission to use my mailbox. It will really be interesting to see what some of those go-for-show Christians do. Let's go see how greedy they are, Missy."

Mrs. Clover and Gabey went inside to the dining table. Gabey made a list of who sent money and how much. $673.00! Gabey was delighted. Mrs. Clover stuffed the empty envelopes into the trash, and Gabey put the money in a grocery sack.

"There may be more come in," Mrs. Clover said. Gabey said she hoped so and headed home to stuff the money in her dictionary.

"No one looks in my dictionary but me," she thought.

Not having $700.00, she sat down and wrote a letter to the Fairview Eye Clinic.

> *Dear Doctor,*
>
> *I am sending you a money order for $673.00 lay-away for a $700.00 glass eye for Loretta Jones of 415 East Washington Street, Dispatch, Oklahoma. Please do not tell her where this comes from. Send her a gift certificate or letter so that she can claim her new eye.*
>
> *Thank you,*
>
> *Gabrieletta Hargus*
> *c/o Mrs. Clover*
> *128 Pierce Street*
> *Dispatch, Oklahoma*
>
> *P.S. I'll get the rest of the money to you right away. If she gets a $500.00 eye, send back the remainder.*

Gabey was counting on a few more dollars to arrive at Mrs. Clover's. There was $10.55 in her piggy bank and she could always babysit. Maybe she could get a job when school was out. Maybe Loretta would choose a $500.00 glass eye. After all, Loretta's eyes weren't very big. She was glad she had been secretive. Her dad would never know. She was sure of it.

Luff Hargus was sitting in the church office completely absorbed in Genesis 38, trying to figure out why such a passage was even in the Bible. He hoped to get to go to Bible college for proper training some day. "One thing about it," he thought, "those ancient Hebrews wrote it all down, no holds barred. Honesty was the lesson, perhaps, or was it duty?"

His meditation was interrupted by a loud banging on the door. Mr. Hargus opened it. There stood Mona Pyle, fresh from the beauty shop with crimps abounding, and red in the face despite the powder.

"What is it, Mona?" he asked softly.

"That kid of yours is headed for the reform school, Luff Hargus."

"You better go over that again. What are you talkin' about?" Luff said, bristling.

"Mail fraud! That's what I'm talking about. A few days ago, we got this letter (which she poked at him). It's about some so-called investments in Futures Unlimited. Some of us got curious and after a little investigating, we found out your daughter is putting the squeeze on all us church members," Mrs. Pyle said, raising her head up high.

Luff read the notice, breathed out a heavy sigh, folded the pamphlet and put it in the pocket of his blue denim workshirt.

"How much did you lose, Mona?" he asked, taking out his billfold.

"That's not the point! I happen to know the sheriff is on his way to your house with legal papers."

"Well, I'll look into it, Mona," he said authoritatively.

When Luff arrived home, Mildred was crying. "The sheriff was here. He left a summons for us to appear in court. Oh, Luff! How could Gabey do such a thing?"

Luff sat down at the kitchen table. "I don't know. To

save my soul, I don't know." he said. "Mona Pyle was by to see me. Maybe I push too hard on Gabey and expect too much. I don't see her enough to help guide her. We wind up arguing. Well, that does it. I'll resign the pulpit."

Mildred Hargus stood at the kitchen sink. Two tears rolled down her cheeks. Luff Hargus laid his head on his hands and sought the wisdom of God Who seemed mighty silent at the moment. Gabey burst through the screen door on the run.

"Mom, I'm going over to Mrs. Clover's, okay?" Gabey called.

"No, you're not, young lady. Get in here," Mildred said sharply.

Gabey entered the back door. She saw her mother's red eyes and her dad's drawn and worried look.

"Who died?" she asked. They only looked like that when somebody died or was in awful trouble.

"Gabey, explain what this is about," Luff said, pulling the letter from his pocket.

"Oh," said Gabey flatly. She tried to act matter-of-factly.

"That—um-m-m. I was trying to raise money, by myself, for something. A good cause."

"This is mail fraud. Illegal procurement of funds," her daddy exclaimed sternly, slapping the paper with the back of his hand.

"I've seen stuff like that in newspaper ads. What's illegal about mine?"

"You can't make good on these promises."

"Oh, I know. I don't have to. I'm going on faith," she explained smilingly. "It's all okay."

"Faith doesn't work like that," Luff said angrily.

"Why not, Daddy. You are always saying the just live by faith and go from faith to faith. This is my first try at it. It is working pretty good. The money has come in better than I thought it would." Her calmness and erroneous use of "faith" irritated him. Luff gritted his teeth.

"How much money, Gabey? Just how much money have you conned this town for? At least, I hope it's just this town."

"I've got $673.00. I only sent that letter in this town and only to people in our church who believe in faith and heaven and stuff," Gabey replied. She hoped Bible talk would win him over.

"Six hundred seventy-three dollars! Great Je-hossaphat! Where is the money now? Do you still have it?"

"No. I spent it, and I can't tell you on what."

Luff Hargus groaned.

"You have to get the money back, Gabey. Get it back and now! You are going to give the people their money back. Every red cent. Do you understand? Do whatever it takes. Do you hear me?" he fairly shouted. Mrs. Hargus could not stand the broken peace of their home and the mounting tension.

"Luff, hold your voice down," Mildred cautioned, touching him gently on the shoulder. "Gabey, do as your father says. Go get the money back."

"But I ordered something," Gabey objected.

"Then call and cancel the thing," her mother demanded, quietly and intensely. "You go right now and cancel your order," Mrs. Hargus said, pointing to the phone, "and Sunday morning, you'll apologize to the people of the church for your misdoing."

Gabey went to the telephone, raised the receiver, and asked for long distance information. She whispered, "I can't buy that eye. My folks won't let me. Can you send it back to the factory? Thanks." She retreated to her bedroom, took the Bible and placed it on the floor. Her folk were furious. The church members were furious. Angelina was gone. It was a sign, to Gabey's understanding, that she was accountable for her actions — no more free rides with God. Slowly, she untied her shoes, pulled off her socks and stood, reverently, on the Bible. "God, help," she said. She simply couldn't think of another thing to say for a time, so she just stood there. "I'm sorry, but I don't know what I've done wrong. Show me," she finally added. Then she cried, thinking no one understood her and that she goofed every time she tried to do good things. Listening to her daddy clinking and clanking on someone's old, worn-out car, she realized she was back where she started — no penance, and worse, no more free rides with God.

Luff Hargus took the text of his pastoral message from Ephesians 6:7 on something about serving the Lord whole-heartedly. Gabey, not wanting to hear her dad preach at her, let her eyes wander across the page to Ephesians 4:28: "He who has been stealing must steal no more, but must work, doing something useful with his own hands, that he may have something to share with those in need."

"I did not really earn that $673.00 myself. That is where my penance was wrong. I have to earn it." Gabey thought. Her attention was not on her father's words until she heard him say "resign." Suddenly, she snapped to attention.

"Therefore," Luff said, "I feel bound to tell you that I'm ready to step down as pastor of this church. I've neglected my own household. I've leaned hard on my Gabey. Instead of being there to help Mildred train her and enjoy her childhood, I've been too busy elsewhere. After the Lord, a man's obligation is to his own household. I've failed both. Mildred and I plan to work on that together."

Gabey used to wish her daddy was anything but a part-time preacher. But now, it sickened her to the core that he was resigning, and it was all her fault. She was causing him embarrassment—it stung and hurt her. In a flash, she realized that she had always been jealous, thinking her daddy's favorite thing was to stand up and preach.

"He is quitting because he wants to spend more time with me," she realized. "He thinks it's his fault. I'm the one who's done the wrong things."

"I believe Gabey has something to say, as well. Gabey?" Her daddy called. Gabey's ears burned. Her hands shook a little. She walked to the front of the church resolved not to make excuses for herself. When she turned around, she saw Jesse Wash sitting in the far, back corner pew. She was encouraged and pleased.

"Your money will be returned right away. I'm sorry I upset everyone. But my daddy is a good person and has knocked his heart and brains out to preach good. He is the closest thing to the out-loud voice of God you have. It's not his fault I didn't understand what he said. It's my fault. So don't worry, you'll get your money back. If he never stands behind another pulpit, that's okay. His life preaches louder than his mouth." She grabbed her daddy and hugged him. They held on to each other until the church was empty.

Luff Hargus looked down tenderly at Gabey. "We have to go before the federal judge tomorrow in Fairview. Can you handle that?" Luff asked Gabey.

"Yes," she said, "I'm not going to jail without a fight."

# CHAPTER 8

## *Plethora of P's*

Judge Mather's courtroom was unusually full. The curious ones, who had heard about the mail fraud charges, were there. Most of the people from the church who had received the fraudulent letter were there. Mona Pyle sat on the front row fanning with a free funeral home fan Mr. Smith was supplying outside of the courthouse. Beak's dad, Mr. Johnson, was there with a pen and pad to gather the news. Gabey had not expected a crowd. It unnerved her. Luff Hargus patted Gabey's shoulder.

It was not to be a trial, but an inquiry, as Gabey understood. She was supposed to tell the judge the truth and the judge would render a decision. They had to wait since two other cases preceded theirs. When the judge came in, the bailiff had everyone stand. The judge banged a gavel which echoed through the chambers, and everyone sat down. It was hard for Gabey to understand everything, because they talked fast like they had all said the words a hundred times before, all cut and dried like a memorized script. The judge said "guilty" to both contenders, and banged the gavel. Gabey jumped. She did not like the gavel banging. "Pay the court clerk on your way out," said the judge. "Next case."

The bailiff, who Gabey decided was the judge's helper, handed some papers to the judge. Mildred Hargus gave her daughter a brief hug.

"Gabrieletta Hargus?" the bailiff called.

"Here, Your Honor," Gabey replied.

"You may approach the bar," Judge Mather invited. Gabey walked forward toward an indoor sort of fence rail, which she guessed was a bar and stood stiff-legged before the judge.

"State your name, please."

"Gabrieletta Hargus. But I'm mostly called Gabey. It rhymes with 'maybe.'"

"How old are you?"

"I'm eleven and a half."

"A parent or guardian is present?"

"Yes, sir."

"The record of complaint states that you used a public facility, namely, the Postal Service, to raise funds for your own gain by selling shares in an alleged business venture, promising up to 300 percent guaranteed return. Is this correct?"

"Partly, Your Honor."

"Which part is incorrect?"

"Raising funds illegally for my ownself." Gabey chewed on her lower lip. The judge thought she was shy, not knowing Gabey was just thinking hard.

"Let's hear your explanation, and I'll sort out the illegalities, if any. Don't be afraid, and be sure to tell the truth."

"Well, Your Honor, I saw in an old copy of the 'Dispatch' that investment firms advertised shares for sale in businesses and real estate projects. I needed some money for a good cause, so I invented a company, too. I decided to name my company 'Future Investments Unlimited' since I was only offering Christians a chance to invest in the Kingdom of Heaven."

Abrupt bursts of laughter erupted in the court room.

Judge Mather banged his gavel to restore dignified quiet to the halls of justice.

"Continue, please," he instructed. "On what grounds did you offer these investments in the Kingdom of Heaven, and how did you intend to pay the dividends?"

"The Bible in I Corinthians 9 says that we reap what we sow. It also says somewhere else — oh — Matthew 13:23, God will return to some thirty times, and, to some even more, up to 100 times what they put into the venture. So I didn't have to pay. God has promised to pay. I just went on faith." She was beginning to feel more confident, even leaned on one foot. "There is a plethora of perspicacious promises waiting for partakers in faith."

Many of Luff Hargus's flock of church goers shifted and squirmed in their seats. Mr. and Mrs. Hargus were astounded at Gabey's story.

"Why did you not state that in your letter?"

"Judge, some people in Dispatch don't even pay the bills they owe to my daddy for working on their old cars. How could I count on those prevaricating prodigals to help me perpetuate and perpetrate precious provender, let alone do a good deed project?" Gabey replied. Judge Mather got lost in Gabey's "P" words but could see guilt written all over some of the citizens. Mr. Johnson held his mouth to keep from laughing. Father Andrew pulled at his collar. Mildred Hargus shut her eyes and wrung her hanky. Mona Pyle fanned harder sending curls flying up and down in front of her ears.

"Was Mrs. Clover involved in the project? Her address is on the letter you sent."

"No. Not really. I borrowed her address."

"Yes, I was involved, Donnie Mather." Mrs. Clover said, rising spryly to her feet in the middle of the fourth row. She called him "Donnie Mather" because she had known him all his life. "I told Gabey she could use my mailbox, and don't you pound that gavel at me, either. Folks in Luff's church and other churches, too, do as little as gets 'em by."

"Mrs. Clover, please, in all due respect to your age and good intentions, please refrain from speaking out in the court room," Judge Mather said politely, but he did not bang his gavel.

"Miss Hargus," the judge continued, "what exactly is this project for which you were gathering monies?"

"Is it relevant to the case, Your Honor?" she asked.

"Yes!" he answered. Then flustered, he said, "I'll ask the questions. The court must know in order to establish intent."

"May I say it so softly that only you hear what I say?" Gabey asked. Judge Mather pursed his lips and rubbed his chin. "I suppose I can allow that. Step closer."

Gabey told the judge she wanted to buy a glass eye, as an act of penance, for slapping a girl her own age. "But I can't now, because my folks already made me promise to give the money back, and they didn't know what I was doing, so don't blame them, Judge, please." Gabey returned to her original spot in front of the bench.

"Where is the money at present?" he asked.

"In the mail. It is all being returned. They should all have it back today or tomorrow."

"Is there anything more you want to say on your behalf before I make a decision, Miss Hargus?" Gabey stood tall as she could, pulled her neck way up high and began her statement.

"Well, I did not mean to make trouble. I did stuff right out of the Bible. And I thought courts respected the Bible as a paragon of justice — the basis of all courtly erudition, and they swear people in using the Bible. Besides, the money is being returned, which, I hope, will exonerate me from the injustice of certain provincial self-appointed judges, Your Honor. Thank you, sir."

Many in the court clapped until the gavel banged several times. Judge Mather shuffled papers on the desk. "She'll either wind up as a lexicographer — or a lawyer," he thought. Lifting his chin a little to compensate for the bifocal lenses in his glasses, he reread Gabey's letter of solicitation. Then he laid the letter aside, took off his glasses and tapped the temple piece lightly on the desk top. Mona Pyle quit fanning and craned her neck forward. One might have thought she was trying to hear Judge Mather's thoughts.

Mr. Johnson of the Dispatch newspaper, sat grinning, chewing the end of his pencil. He was going to have fun writing this item. Father Andrew recrossed his legs. Mrs. Clover was twiddling her thumbs, remembering when Donnie Mather use to hide on her front porch from a neighborhood bully, and recalled the day when Donnie stood up for himself. Mr. Smith was so still, he appeared to neither blink nor breathe. He was the only one looking cool that hot day. Mildred and Luff Hargus held on to each other's hands. Someone coughed. Gabey stood on one foot and then the other.

After a long and uncomfortable silence, Judge Mather ceased pondering, and looked across the court room. "The law of this country is based on the Constitution. The Constitution is based on the noble principles contained in the Bible upon which you", shifting his gaze to Gabey, "claim to have based your actions. It contains great wisdom. Wisdom of Moses, the Psalmist, Solomon and others. However, your methods of living by the noble principles herein are unorthodox, exhibit lack of discernment, and are not completely above board due to the secrecy of your own private goal, albeit a very worthy, unselfish one. It was a misleading letter." Gabey cringed.

"The recipients were overcome by a desire to turn a quick profit in this enterprise, having no idea they were actually being called upon to invest in a heavenly kingdom. Therein lies the fault. You misled them by not telling the truth as to the whereabouts of the real estate. However, since you have promised to return to them their original investments, I see no cause for further justice to be extracted. No malicious intent of fraud has been detected. Mr. Hargus and Mrs. Hargus, as parents, you will make sure that all the money is returned?"

"We will, Your Honor." Mr. Hargus replied.

"Gabrieletta," the judge gave the briefest smile and whispered, "I wish you well achieving your goal." Then more loudly, "Charges are dismissed. Defendant is directed to pay court costs. Pay the court clerk now upon leaving the chambers."

"Thank you, Judge. Thank you for your discernment," Gabey said.

"All rise," said the bailiff, and the judge left the court room. The Hargus family smiled and hugged.

"I do wish you hadn't said that about folks owing us, Gabey," Luff said.

"Well, you know it's true, Daddy."

"No matter. I was proud of you. Let's go home." Gabey felt right with the world. It felt good to be walking beside her parents — on the same side — agreeing. "Agreement," she thought, "is more than a noun. I'll bet I'm getting more discernment."

Mr. Johnson dashed out to print the juiciest bit of news since the Catholic church had been robbed.

When Gabey arrived home, the first thing she did was write another letter to the Fairview Eye Clinic:

227 Adams Street
*Fairview, Oklahoma*
*May 10, 1950*

*Dear Doctor,*

*I'm sorry to bother you again, but I hope you will send a glass eye to Loretta Jones, 415 E. Washington St., Dispatch, Oklahoma. I promise to pay the bill at $4.00 a month, if it takes me the rest of my life. Please let me hear from you soon.*

*Sincerely,*

*Gabrieletta Hargus*

*P.S. If I win the chamber of commerce prize on Dispatch's history, I'll send you $25.00 right away.*

Gabey could scarcely wait for school. The paper, based on Mrs. Clover's interesting recollections, was her best composition yet. Surely, it stood a good chance to win. She arrived at school totally unprepared for the crowd that gathered and the barrage of questions about her day in court.

"Did they throw you in jail?" "Did you get the third degree?" "Did they shine a light in your eyes?" "Blow smoke in your face?" The students pushed and pulled her this way and that. She could not answer. "Were you really your own lawyer?" "Did you really get $1,000 from your scheme?" The questioning continued after the bell for class. Gabey tried to explain but they wouldn't listen. The students crowded and pressed in from all sides, even down the hall and into the room. The rumors were ridiculous. Gabey could not imagine how they got started so quickly.

Mrs. Moss had a hard time settling the students. "Please, let Gabey alone. She has probably heard enough of your questions for the time being. It is time for class and we have important business."

Gabey could have kissed her.

"Now I know you all are eager to hear who the

winner of the Chamber of Commerce's writing contest is. Runner-up is Beak Johnson for the architecture of Dispatch. He gets this nice Esterbrook fountain pen. Congratulations, Beak!" Mrs. Moss said. The applause was enthusiastic. Beak stuck his chin out and grinned. He was clearly surprised and had not counted on winning anything.

"And now I would like you to join with me in congratulating the winner — Loretta Jones — with her entry on 'Commerce and Industry in Dispatch,'" Mrs. Moss stated.

LORETTA? Gabey was absolutely stunned. Loretta never got more than B's in composition. Gabey's disbelief faded into despair. Everything she had tried to do for weeks and weeks had failed, backfired, or flopped. Gabey hurt way down deep. What chamber of commerce would want to tell the world a goofy story about their town being won in a horse race and blessed by an old Negro hobo who might have been an angel? "How could I have been so dumb?" she wondered.

Gabey had no desire to play ball with Beak and his friends at recess, but she did. During afternoon classes, she worked the lessons automatically, quietly doing what was put before her to do.

When the bell rang, she left for home. Beak hurried to catch up with her. He was afraid she was upset because he won something and she did not. She did not even get honorable mention in the writing contest. Then too, she could be mad because his father had written a funny article about her "day in court"; her use of $2.00 words on a fifty-cent charge and about it raining "P's" in Fairview.

Beak had read the paper and thought Gabey was as good as Perry Mason. She was gutsy, too, facing up to that judge and half the town by herself.

"Gabey," he hollered, "Wait up." Gabey paused. "You aren't mad at me, are you?" he asked.

"No, Idjit. Should I be?" she asked flatly.

"I did get second in the contest. I thought you would win, though."

"Bet you wish that fountain pen was a pair of baseball shoes."

"No."

"No? I thought you wanted new baseball shoes," Gabey said.

"I got some —," he paused, and then added, '— from Jesse Wash." Beak dropped his eyes.

"Jesse Wash? Why did he give you new shoes?" she asked.

"Well, I might as well tell you. It's time I came clean, I guess. I was walking by the Catholic church one day, and the door was open. I went to peek in and I saw some silver candlesticks on a table at the entry. I stuffed them in my duffel bag with my baseball duds."

"You didn't!"

"Yeah, I did. Jesse saw me take them. He was hauling off limbs from across the street. When I was at the park, he asked me about it. I felt rotten about stealing. Thought I'd hock them in Fairview for baseball shoes. He drove me to the church to take them back, then he showed me those new pitches. The strange thing is — those baseball shoes were delivered the next day in the mail with a card that said, 'For a promising player.' It had to be Jesse. Dad and Mom acted as surprised as I was, unless they were just foolin', and I don't think they were."

"That explains why you were such a snot when I told you Jesse is an angel. He's probably your angel. We've got to watch him to find out," Gabey replied.

"I still say he's straight out of prison. Probably a bum rap, though. Anyway, that's why I wanted to know that day when you were going to the Catholic church. I was afraid you'd found out or would. Then you really scared me with all that angel talk. Do I still have to wait until I'm ninety years old? What is going on?"

"No, I'll tell you, but keep quiet about it. Daddy wanted me to do penance for slapping Loretta. I was afraid he'd lose his church and that I'd go to hell if I didn't confess and get things right and try to do right. That's why I wanted you to ask Loretta if she'd like to have a glass eye. I hurt her feelings calling her the 'one-eyed thing'. Father Andrew says people become accountable for their actions around the age of twelve, or whenever they get discernment—because God gives us a free ride until we are old enough to know better and even sends angels to watch over children. After that, you are on your own.

"So I went to the church to confess, after I looked up penance in the dictionary and found out that confessing is part of penance. But when I found out glass eyes cost a gob of dough, I nearly fainted. That is when I made up that scheme for heavenly investment that landed me in court. But I'm not done yet, Beak. I've re-ordered an eye for Loretta. I'll be paying all my allowance forever on that eye, if the doctor will let me pay it off. And you'd better not tell anyone about this—ever," Gabey ended.

"What if Loretta doesn't want an eye?" Beak asked.

"She can give it back to the doctor in Fairview. But I'm going to give her one, whether she wants it or not. That's my penance. What she does with it is her business. I just hope when I get home that I have the doctor's answer in the mail."

# CHAPTER 9

## *Payments and Promises*

Gabey found her mother at the dining table opening a letter from a large pile of mail.

"What is all this?" Gabey asked.

Mildred laughed. "Letters to you. Letters to us. The ones to us are mostly people paying bills they've owed your dad so long we'd even forgotten."

"Good. I still think Daddy should send out bills. Everyone else does," said Gabey, digging through her stack for a letter from the eye doctor. (Luff Hargus had never kept records nor sent out bills. He thought a car that ran was a good enough reminder.)

"No letter," Gabey sighed.

A knock came at the door, "Anyone home?" It was Mona Pyle. Mildred asked her in and sent Gabey to get her daddy out from under a car where he was replacing a tail pipe.

"I've been sent, Pastor; no, I volunteered, actually, to tell you the church would like for you to stay on as pastor. In fact, we've taken up a collection for you to enroll in one of them courses at the Bible college."

Luff Hargus laughed right out loud, then he did something no one had ever seen him do before. He threw both arms around Mona Pyle, lifted her off the floor and twirled her around. Mona was so stunned, she left the house without a word. Mildred laughed, hugged her husband and laughed some more. Luff kissed his wife right in front of Gabey. Gabey had never seen him kiss her smack on the mouth before. She stared bug-eyed. The phone rang. Gabey left her parents in the kitchen and reluctantly answered it.

"Hello."

"Miss Gabrieletta Hargus?"

"Yes. I'm Gabey."

"This is Doctor Martin, Fairview Eye Clinic. I want to thank you for your confidence in us as eye surgeons. We also appreciate your concern for the health needs of others. I also wanted you to know that we have contacted the school nurse at Dispatch, and Loretta Jones will be coming for an examination when school is out. The nurse's information leads us to believe Loretta is a good candidate for simple eye surgery which may restore her vision — at least, we hope so. The only cost to you would be $125.00 for extra hospital costs and medication, since patrons of our clinic have a fund for such needy children as Loretta. We'll be glad to let you pay it out at $4.00 a month. How does that sound?"

"That will be fine by me, Dr. Martin. Just don't tell Loretta, okay?"

"I wouldn't dream of it. Say, I read about you in the Fairview Times. You're quite a young lady. My hat is off to you."

"Thanks, doctor. Thanks a lot. You'll never now how profoundly grateful I am." Gabey hung up the phone.

"Yippee!" she yelled to the top of her lungs.

"Luff, that must have been Dr. Martin talking to Gabey," Mildred remarked.

"I reckon so. I told him she'd be home about 4:00 o'clock. Bede Martin. I remember fixin' his busted radiator when he drove through here to enroll in medical school. He paid me off a few dollars now and then. I told him to go to Joe Claire and trade that sorry car off."

"Yes, I remember him." Mildred replied.

"He called me this morning and read me Gabey's letter. It just about got me. He wanted to take up the whole cost, but I told him 'no.' He finally agreed not to steal her thunder. I figured it was her penance. That's what this whole mess has been about—her penance—my doing. She's taken quite a whippin'—the last whipping from me."

"Yes, she has," Mildred agreed. "Now, come help me rearrange the living room, if you still intend to buy a TV set tomorrow."

Gabey ran next door. "Beak! Hey, Beak!" she yelled from the yard.

"Yeah?" he answered, and came outside carrying a bowl of ice cream. "What's up?"

"I'm out of my jam. Let's get our bikes and stake a lookout on Jesse Wash. I've got a plan."

"Oh no! Never! Nay! Are you nuts?"

"No, Idjit. I just have a palpable penchant for pursuing adventures," Gabey replied. "Coming?"

"Nah. I'm going to watch 'Wild Adventure' on TV."

"Wouldn't you rather be in an adventure than watch one? You know your problem, Beak? You're all wound up in those negative 'n' words. 'P' is for positive."

"Yeah? Well, 'p' is for penitentiary where they send you for breaking the law, and they lock you up in a hot box in the prison yard with no water. Your tongue swells up and turns black when you've sweated out all your sweat. Then your skin peels off."

"That's a lie, Beak. Did you see that on TV?"

"Ask Jesse Wash if it's a lie. I'll bet he's a convict."

"I'll bet you a dollar he's an angel—not a convict."

"A whole dollar?"

"Yeah. And you'll just have to take my word for it, if you don't go with me to check him out."

"You won't do something stupid and get us in trouble, will you?"

"Why, Beacon Johnson. What makes you think I'd get us in trouble?"

Beak's stomach knotted, but he rolled out of the drive on his bike anyway, wary of the grin on Gabey's face.

"Okay, Beak—let's go find us an angel."